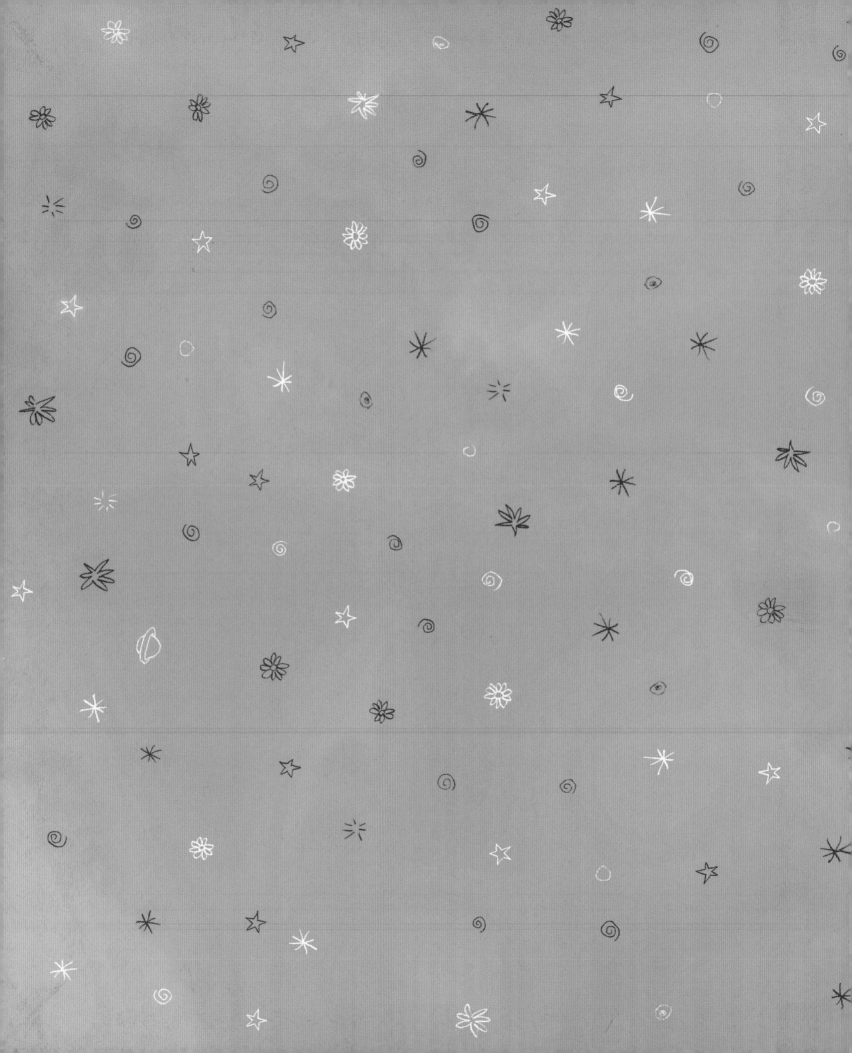

For Harry, Katie (the real one), Lily and Ben, and for
my godchildren Isabelle and Archie. I love you all! — J. H.

To Isa — F. S.

tiger tales
5 River Road, Suite 128, Wilton, CT 06897
Published in the United States 2015
Originally published in Great Britain 2015
by Little Tiger Press
Text copyright © 2015 Jenna Harrington
Illustrations copyright © 2015 Finn Simpson
ISBN-13: 978-1-58925-192-2
ISBN-10: 1-58925-192-X
Printed in China
LTP/1800/1137/0315

For more insight and activities, visit us at www.tigertalesbooks.com

Katie McGinty Wants a Pet!

by
Jenna Harrington

Illustrated by
Finn Simpson

tiger tales

Katie McGinty wanted a pet.
She wanted a pet more than ANYTHING in the world.

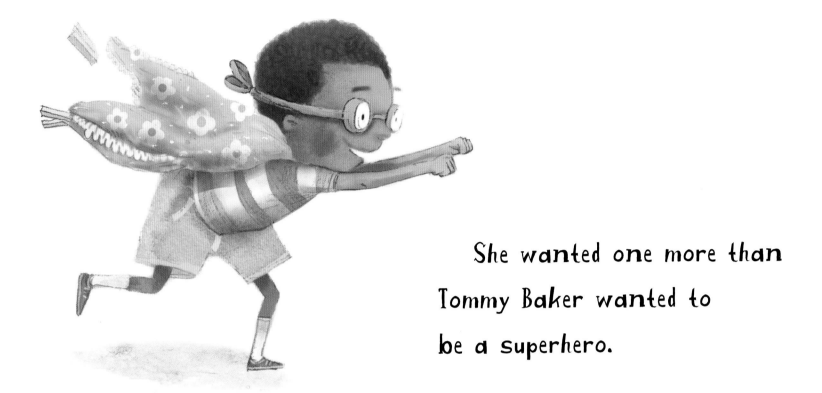

She wanted one more than
Tommy Baker wanted to
be a superhero.

More than Molly Phillips
wanted to be able to
stand on her head . . .

... and more than Hannah Hobbs
wished she had a sister.

But Daddy told Katie she had
to wait until she was a big girl.
So Katie waited, and measured herself every day . . .

. . . until finally, she WAS big enough!

Katie was so excited that she dragged Daddy down the street.
"Slow down, Katie," said Daddy, "and tell me
what kind of pet you want."

You have
to guess!

"Um . . .
is it a hamster?"
asked Daddy.

No!

"How about a cat?"
he said.

No!

"I know!" Daddy cried. "You want a dog like Grandma's."

No!

A chipmunk? A snake? A pig?

No! No! No!

"What I would like more than anything in the world," laughed Katie, "is a . . ."

"...ZEBRA!"

Daddy shook his head in disbelief. "I'm sorry, Katie, but you can't have a zebra as a pet. They live in Africa where it's hot. It's much too cold here."

"That's okay, Daddy," said Katie. "Grandma can knit him a nice warm sweater, and he can wear Mommy's slippers on his feet."

"Hmm . . . but you just can't buy zebras in a pet shop," said Daddy. "Besides, what would we feed him? We only have a small yard, and there's not much grass for him to eat."

Katie shook her head.

"Don't be silly, Daddy!" she giggled. "He'll eat pizza, and fish sticks, and spaghetti with us at the table, of course!"

"And I suppose he would have to sleep in the garage?" Daddy asked.

"Don't be silly, Daddy! He's going to sleep in my room in the bunk bed with me," Katie said happily.

"In your bunk bed?" Daddy scratched his head.

"And will he take a bath with you, too?" he asked.
Katie laughed. "Don't be silly, Daddy . . ."

". . . the tub is much too small.
I'll have to wash him in the swimming pool!"

"Katie, we are almost at the pet shop," said Daddy. "I know you really want a zebra, but I'm afraid you just can't have one."

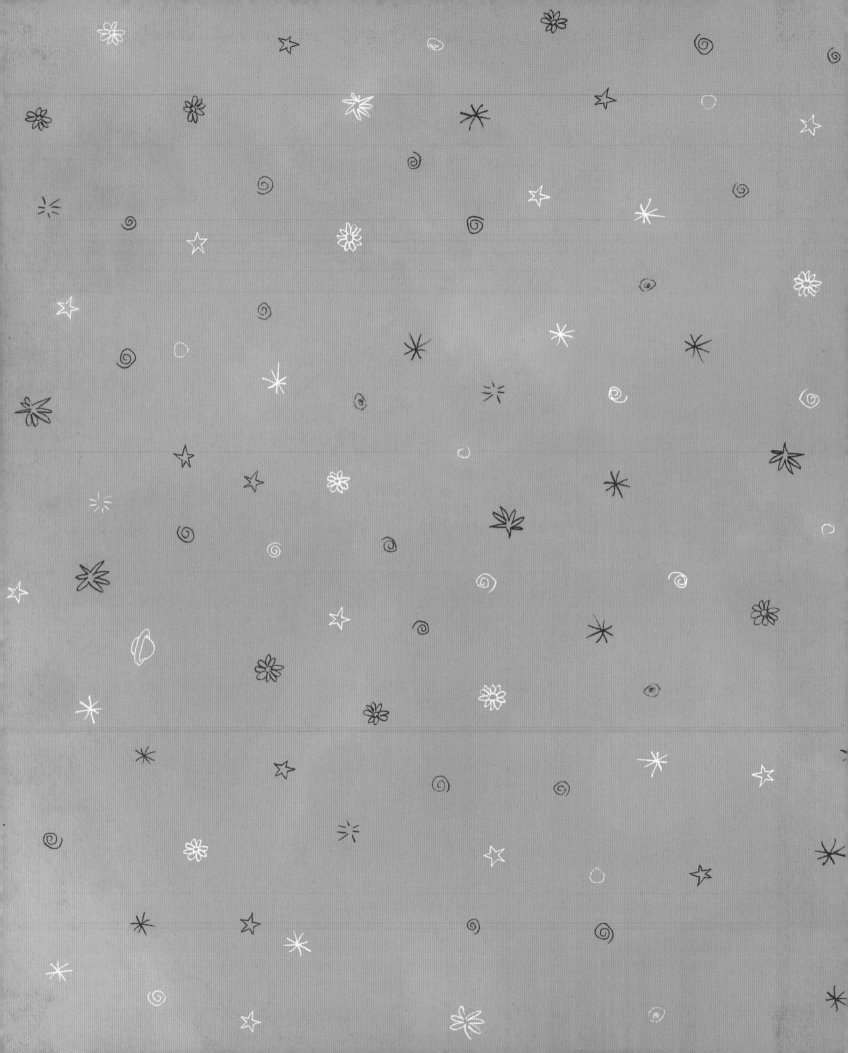